Digger to the Rescue

Mandy Archer

Illustrated by Martha Lightfoot

NEW
BURLINGTON
BOOKS

Bear arrives **early** for work.
Digger is ready and waiting!

It's going to be a **busy** day
on the building site.

The foreman checks his plans. They are building an **adventure playground**.

There are lots of **jobs** for Digger.

Bear puts his foot on Digger's step.
He SWINGS UP to the driver's seat.

Bear sits in the **driver's seat.**

He **turns** the ignition key and **steps on** the pedals.

VROOM!
VROOM!

Digger **chugs** through the building site.

Bear **swivels** his seat around and **pulls**
the lever to lower Digger's scoop.

Stabilizers stop Digger tipping over.

Digger **needs** to make a hole so the foundations can be laid. Sharp teeth **dig** into the earth.

Bear **SCOOPS** up giant mounds
of earth using Digger's bucket.

V-R-R-ROOM!

The earth is dropped into the dump truck.

Time for Digger's **next** job!

The road roller needs to **flatten** the ground for the tarmac to be laid.

First, Digger needs to clear the **rubble**.

After lunch it's time for an engine check.
Bear **fills** Digger with **diesel**, then
he checks the **water** and **oil**.

The foreman **ticks** his clipboard.

He gives Bear and Digger a **thumbs-up.**

Everything is okay so it's back to work!

Digger works hard **all afternoon.**
Suddenly Bear's cell phone rings.

Children from
the nearby
school have
spotted a
cat stuck
in a tree!

Can Digger help?

Bear drives Digger over to the edge
of the building site.

BEEP!

BEEP!

BEEP!

Warning lights
flash and beep.
Stand back,
everyone!

The metal arm **rises UP** and gently Bear edges Digger's **bucket** toward the tree.

The schoolchildren watch **quietly.**

Bear positions the bucket **next to** the branch.

The cat **peers** in nervously...

...and then jumps into the bucket!

The children **cheer**.
Digger is a **hero**!

Bear grins. He **carefully** **lowers** the bucket to the ground.

Digger is covered in **mud** and needs
a **wash** and a **scrub**.

Soon it looks as
good as new.

What a day! Bear drives Digger
back toward the yard.

Bear **turns off** the ignition, and
Digger's engine **splutters** to a stop.

Bear climbs out of the cab. Good work, Digger. See you in the morning!

Let's look at
Digger

Levers

Bucket

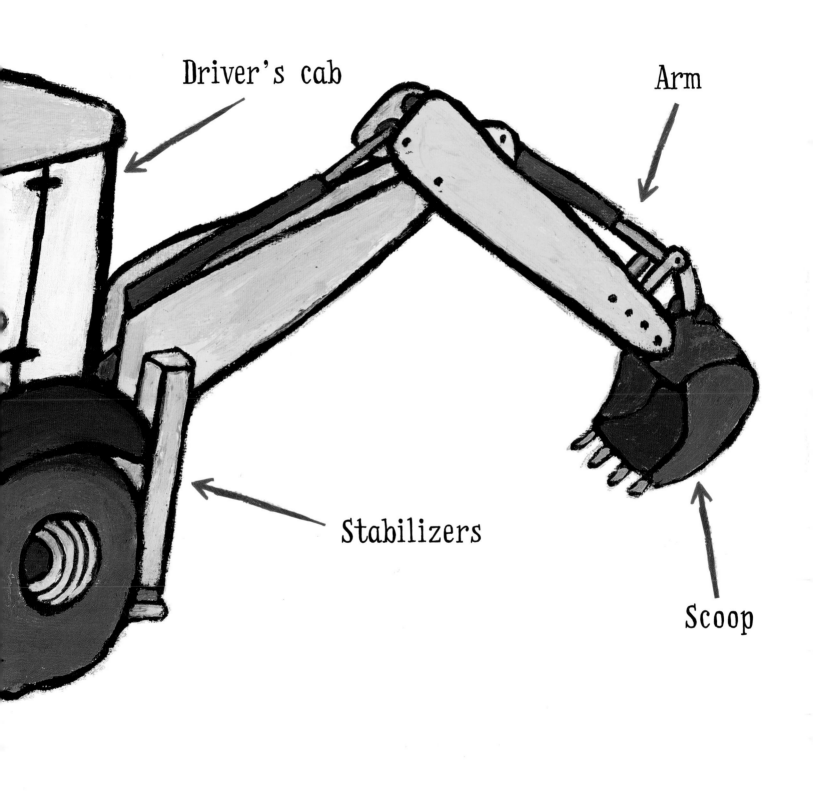

Driver's cab

Arm

Stabilizers

Scoop

Other Building Machines

Road roller

Dump truck

Crane

Bulldozer

For Will, Anna, and Sam M.L.

A NEW BURLINGTON BOOK
The Old Brewery
6 Blundell Street
London N7 9BH

Designer: Plum Pudding Design

Copyright © QEB Publishing 2012

First published in the United States in 2012 by
QEB Publishing, Inc.
3 Wrigley, Suite A
Irvine, CA 92618

www.qed-publishing.co.uk

A CIP record for this book is available from the Library of Congress.

ISBN: 978 1 78171 389 1

Printed in China